PUFFIN BOOKS

CHAIR PERSON

The old armchair has been sitting in front of the television for as long as Simon and Marcia can remember. But it has never been very comfortable, and is now so old and worn that Mum and Dad decide it is time to replace it with a new one. It will make a good seat for the guy on bonfire night.

But the chair itself has other ideas. To the amazement and growing alarm of the family the discarded chair takes on a life of its own and Chair Person, as he calls himself, settles in as an uninvited guest.

He speaks oddly and is terribly clumsy, but at first seems friendly, so that the children do their best to make him feel at home. But soon they regret their hospitality as Chair Person's behaviour gets worse and worse. His manners are appalling and his demands outrageous. No one seems able to control him. The whole family is plunged into chaos and the search for a solution becomes increasingly desperate – perhaps Auntie Christa will be able to help?

Diana Wynne Jones was brought up in the country. She has written a number of children's books, in which she has used events from her own childhood. She is married to an Oxford don and has three sons.

CHAIR PERSON

by

DIANA WYNNE JONES

Illustrated by Glenys Ambrus

PUFFIN BOOKS

PUFFIN BOOKS

Published by the Penguin Group
27 Wrights Lane, London w8 5tz, England
Viking Penguin Inc., 40 West 23rd Street, New York, New York 10010, USA
Penguin Books Australia Ltd, Ringwood, Victoria, Australia
Penguin Books Canada Ltd, 2801 John Street, Markham, Ontario, Canada l3r 1b4
Penguin Books (NZ) Ltd, 182–190 Wairau Road, Auckland 10, New Zealand

Penguin Books Ltd, Registered Offices: Harmondsworth, Middlesex, England

First published by Hamish Hamilton Children's Books 1989
Published in Puffin Books 1991
10 9 8 7 6 5 4 3 2 1

Made and printed in Great Britain by
Richard Clay Ltd., Bungay, Suffolk
Filmset in Baskerville (Linotron 202)

Chapter 1

WHAT HAPPENED TO the old striped armchair was Auntie Christa's fault.

The old chair had stood in front of the television for as long as Simon and Marcia could remember. As far as they knew, the cushion at the top had always been tipped sideways and it had never been comfortable to sit in. The seat was too short for Dad and too low for Mum and too high for Simon or Marcia. Its arms were the wrong shape for putting things on. Perhaps that was why there was a coffee-stain on one arm and a blot of ink on the other. There was a sticky brown patch on the seat where Simon and Marcia had once had a fight for the ketchup bottle. Then one evening, the sideways cushion at the top wore out. Whatever the chair was stuffed with began to ooze out in a spiky brown bush.

"The armchair's grown a beard," said Simon.

"It looks as if someone's smashed a hedgehog on it," Marcia said.

Dad stood and looked at it. "Let's get rid of it," he said. "I've never liked it, anyway. I tell you what – we can sit the guy in it on Guy Fawkes night. That will make a really good bonfire."

Marcia thought this was a very good idea. Now she thought about it, she had never liked that chair either. The purple and orange and pale blue stripes on it never seemed to go with anything else in the room. Simon was not so sure. He always liked things that he *knew*, and he had known that chair all his life. It seemed a shame to burn it on the bonfire. He was glad when Mum objected.

"Oh, you can't throw it out!" Mum said. "It's got such a personality!"

"But it's worn out," said Dad. "It

3

wasn't new when we bought it. We can afford to buy a much nicer one now."

They argued about it, until Simon began to feel sorry for the old chair and even Marcia felt a little guilty about burning a chair that was old enough to have a personality.

"Couldn't we just sell it?" she asked.

"Don't *you* start!" said Dad. "Even the junk shop wouldn't want a mucky old thing like – "

At that moment, Auntie Christa came in. Auntie Christa was not really an auntie, but she liked everyone to call her that. As usual, she came rushing in through the kitchen, carrying three carrier bags and a cardboard box and calling, "Coo-ee! It's me!" When she arrived in the living room, she sank down into the striped armchair and panted, "I just had to come in. I'm on my way to the Community Hall, but my feet are killing me. I've been all afternoon

collecting prizes for the children's
party for the Caring Society on
Saturday – I must have walked *miles*!
But you wouldn't *believe* what *wonderful*
prizes people have given me. Just
look." She dumped her cardboard box
on the arm of the chair – it was the
arm with the ink blot – in order to
fetch a bright green teddy bear out of
one of the carrier bags. She wagged the
teddy in their faces. "Isn't he
charming?"

"So-so," said Dad and Marcia added, "Perhaps he'd look better without the pink ribbon." Simon and Mum were too polite to say anything.

"And here's such a lovely clockwork train!" Auntie Christa said, plunging the teddy back in the bag and pulling out a broken engine. "Isn't it exciting? I can't stay long enough to show you everything – I have to go and see to the music for the Senior Citizens' Dance in a minute – but I think I've just got time to drink a cup of tea."

"Of course," Mum said guiltily. "Coming up." She dashed into the kitchen.

Auntie Christa was good at getting people to do things. She was a very busy lady. Whatever went on at the Community Hall – whether it was Youth Club Disco, Children's Fancy

Dress, Mothers' Choir, Dog Training, Soup for the Homeless or a Bring and Buy Sale – Auntie Christa was sure to be in the midst of it, telling people what to do. She was usually too busy to listen to what other people said. Mum said Auntie Christa was a wonder, but Dad quite often muttered "Quack-quack-quack" under his breath when Auntie Christa was talking.

"Quack-quack," Dad murmured as Auntie Christa went on fetching things out of her bags and telling them what good prizes they were. Auntie Christa had just got through all the things in the bags and was turning to the cardboard box on the arm of the chair, when Mum came dashing back with tea and biscuits.

"Tea!" Auntie Christa said. "I can

always rely on a cup of tea in this house!"

She turned gladly to take the tea. Behind her, the box slid into the chair.

"Never mind," said Auntie Christa. "I'll show you what's in there in a minute. It will thrill Simon and Marcia – oh, that reminds me! The African Aid Coffee Morning has to be moved this Saturday because the Stamp Collectors need the hall. I think we'll have the coffee morning here instead. You can easily manage coffee and cakes for twenty on Saturday, can't you?" she asked Mum. "Marcia and Simon can help you."

"Well – " Mum began, while Dad looked truly dismayed.

"That's settled, then," said Auntie Christa and quickly went on to talk about other things. Dad and Simon

9

and Marcia looked at one another glumly. They knew they were booked to spend Saturday morning handing round cakes and soothing Mum while she fussed. But it was worse than that.

"Now, you'll never guess what's in the box," Auntie Christa said, cheerily passing her cup for more tea. "Suppose we make it a competition. Let's say that whoever guesses wrong has to come and help me with the Caring Society party on Saturday afternoon."

"I think we'll all be busy – " Dad tried to say.

"No refusing!" Auntie Christa cried. "People are so wicked, the way they always try to get out of doing good deeds! You can have one guess each. And I'll give you a clue. Old Mr Pennyfeather gave me the box."

As old Mr Pennyfeather kept the

junk shop, there could have been almost anything in the box. They all thought rather hard.

Simon thought the box had rattled as it tipped. "A tea-set," he guessed.

Marcia thought she had heard the box slosh. "A goldfish in a bowl," she said.

Mum thought of something that might make a nice prize and guessed, "Dolls' house furniture."

Dad thought of the sort of things that were usually in Mr Pennyfeather's shop and said, "Mixed-up jigsaws."

"You're all wrong, of course!" Auntie Christa said while Dad was still speaking. She sprang up and pulled the box back to the arm of the chair. "It's an old-fashioned conjuror's kit. Look. Isn't it thrilling?" She held up a large black top hat with a big shiny

12

blue ball in it. Water — or something — was dripping out of the hat underneath. "Oh dear," Auntie Christa said. "I think the crystal ball must be leaking. It's made quite a puddle in your chair."

Dark liquid was spreading over the seat of the chair, mixing with the old ketchup stain.

"Are you sure you didn't spill your tea?" Dad asked.

Mum gave him a stern look. "Don't worry," she said. "We were going to throw the chair away, anyway. We were just talking about it when you came."

"Oh good!" Auntie Christa said merrily. She rummaged in the box again. "Look, here's the conjuror's wand," she said, bringing out a short white stick wrapped in a string of little flags. "Let's magic the nasty wet away so that I can sit down again." She tapped the puddle in the chair with the stick. "There!"

"The puddle hasn't gone," said Dad.

"I thought you were going to throw the hideous old thing away, anyway," Auntie Christa said crossly. "You should be quite ashamed to invite people for a coffee morning and ask them to sit in a chair like this!"

"Then perhaps," Dad said politely, "you'd like to help us carry the chair outside to the garden shed?"

"I'd love to, of course," Auntie Christa said, hurriedly putting the hat and the stick back into the box and collecting her bags, "but I must dash. I have to speak to the Vicar before I see about the music. I'll see you all at the Caring Society party the day after tomorrow at four-thirty sharp. Don't forget!"

This was a thing Simon and Marcia had often noticed about Auntie Christa. Though she was always busy, it was always other people who did the hard work.

Chapter 2

NOW MUM HAD told Auntie Christa they were going to throw the chair away, she wanted to do it at once.

"We'll go and get another one tomorrow after work," she told Dad. "A nice blue, I think, to go with the curtains. And let's get this one out of the way now. I'm sick of the sight of it."

It took all four of them to carry the chair through the kitchen to the back door, and they knocked most of the kitchen chairs over doing it. For the

next half hour they thought they were
not going to get it through the back
door. It stuck, whichever way they
tipped it. Simon was quite upset. It
was almost as if the chair was trying to
stop them throwing it away. But they
got it into the garden in the end.
Somehow, as they staggered across the
lawn with it, they knocked the top off
Mum's new sundial and flattened a
rosebush. Then they had to stand it
sideways in order to wedge it inside the
shed.

"There," Dad said, slamming the shed door and dusting his hands. "That's out of the way until Guy Fawkes Day."

He was wrong, of course.

The next day, Simon and Marcia had to collect the key from next door and let themselves into the house, because Mum had gone straight from work to meet Dad and buy a new chair. They felt very gloomy being in the empty house. The living room looked queer with an empty space where the chair had been. And both of them kept remembering that they would have to spend Saturday helping in Auntie Christa's schemes.

"Handing round cakes might be fun," Simon said doubtfully.

"But helping with the party won't be," said Marcia. "We'll have to do all the work. Why couldn't one of us have guessed what was in that box?"

"What *are* Caring Society children, anyway?" asked Simon.

"I *think*," said Marcia, "that they *may* be the ones who have to let themselves into their houses with a key after school."

They looked at one another. "Do you think we count?" said Simon. "Enough to win a prize, anyway. I wouldn't mind winning that conjuring set. It was a real top hat, even if the crystal ball did leak."

Here they both began to notice a distant thumping noise from somewhere out in the garden. It suddenly felt unsafe being alone in the house.

"It's only next door hanging up pictures again," Marcia said bravely.

But when they went rather timidly to listen at the back door, the noise was definitely coming from the garden shed.

"It's next door's dog got shut in the shed again," Simon said. It was his turn to be brave. Marcia was scared of next door's dog. She hung back while Simon marched over the lawn and tugged and pulled until he got the shed door open.

It was not a dog. There was a person standing inside the shed. The person stood and stared at them with his little head on one side. His little fat arms waved about as if he was not sure what to do with them. He breathed in heavy snorts and gasps as if he was not sure how to breathe.

"Er, hn hm," he said as if he was not sure how to speak either. "I appear to have been shut in your shed."

"Oh – *sorry*!" Simon said, wondering
how it had happened.

The person bowed, in a crawlingly
humble way. "I – hn hm – am the one

21

who is snuffle sorry," he said. "I have made – hn hm – you come all the way here to let me out." He walked out of the shed, swaying and bowing from foot to foot.

Simon backed away, wondering if the person walked like that because he had no shoes on. He was a solid, plump person with wide, hairy legs. He was wearing a most peculiar striped one-piece suit that only came to his knees.

Marcia backed away behind Simon, staring at the person's stripy arms. He waved them in a feeble way as he walked. There was a blot of ink on one arm and what looked like a coffee stain on the other. Marcia's eyes went to the person's plump striped stomach. As he came out into the light, she could see that the stripes were sky-blue, orange

22

and purple. There was a damp patch
down the middle and a dark sticky
place that could have been ketchup,
once. Her eyes went up to his sideways
face. There was a beard on the
person's chin that looked rather as if
someone had smashed a hedgehog on
it.

"Who *are* you?" she said.

The person stood still. His arms
waved like seaweed in a current. "Er,
hn hm, I am Chair Person," he said.
His sideways face looked pleased and
rather smug about it.

Marcia and Simon of course both
felt awful about it. He was the
armchair. They had put him in the
shed ready to go on the bonfire. Now
he was alive. They hoped very much
that Chair Person did not know that
they had meant to burn him.

"Won't you come inside?" Simon said politely.

"That is *very* kind of you," Chair Person said, crawlingly humble again. "I – hn hm snuffle – hope that won't be too much trouble."

"Not at all!" they both said heartily.

They went towards the house. Crossing the lawn was quite difficult, because Chair Person did not seem to have learnt to walk straight yet, and he talked all the time. "I believe I am – hn hm – Chair Person," he said, crashing into what was left of the sundial and knocking it down, "because I think I am. Snuffle. Oh dear, I appear to have destroyed your stone pillar."

"Not to worry," Marcia said kindly. "It was broken last night when we – I mean, it was broken anyway."

"Then – hn hm – as I was saying," Chair Person said, veering the other way, "that this is what snuffle wise men say. A person who thinks is a Person." He cannoned into the apple tree. Most of the apples Dad had meant to pick that weekend came showering and bouncing down on to the grass. "Oh dear," said Chair Person. "I appear to have loosened your fruit."

"That's all right," Simon and
Marcia said politely. But since Chair
Person, in spite of seeming so humble,
did not seem very sorry about the
apples and just went on talking and
weaving about, they each took hold of
one of his waving arms and guided him
to the back door.

"Only the finest snuffle apples," said
Chair Person as he bashed into both
sides of the back door, "from the finest
– hn hm – orchards go into Kaplan's
Peasant Pies. This is one of many
snuffle facts I know. Er, hm, very few
people have watched as much
television as I have," he added,
knocking over the nearest kitchen
chair.

Marcia picked the chair up, thinking
of the many, many times she had gone
out of the living room and forgotten to

turn the television off. Chair Person, when he was an armchair, must have watched hours of commercials and hundreds of films.

Simon turned Chair Person round and sat him in the kitchen chair. Chair Person went very humble and grateful. "You are – hn hm – treating me with such kindness," he said, "and I am going to cause you a lot of snuffle trouble. I appear to need something to eat. I am not sure what to do about it. Do I – hn hm – eat *you*?"

"We'll find you something to eat," Simon said quickly.

"Eating people is wrong," Marcia explained.

They hurried to find some food. A tin of spaghetti seemed easiest, because they both knew how to do that. Simon opened the tin and Marcia put it in a

saucepan with the gas very high to get
the spaghetti hot as soon as possible.
Both of them cast nervous looks at
Chair Person in case he tried to eat one
of them. But Chair Person sat where
he was, waving his arms gently. "Hn
hm, Spiggley's tasty snacks," he said.

"Sunshine poured from a tin." When
Marcia put the steaming plateful in
front of him and Simon laid a spoon
and a fork on either side of it, Chair
Person went on sitting and staring.

"You can eat it," Simon said kindly.

"Er, hn hm," Chair Person said.
"But this is not a complete meal. I
shall have to trouble you for a napkin
and salt and pepper. And I think
people usually snuffle eat by candle
light with soft music in the
background."

They hurried to find him the salt,
the pepper mill and a paper towel.
Simon fetched the radio and turned it
on. It was playing Country and
Western, but Simon turned it down
very low and hoped it would do. He
felt so sorry for Chair Person that he
wanted to please him. Marcia ran

upstairs and found the candlesticks
from Mum's dressing table and two
red candles from last Christmas. She
felt so guilty about Chair Person that
she wanted to please him as much as
Simon did.

Chair Person was very humble and
grateful. While he told them how kind
they were being, he picked up the
pepper mill and began solemnly
grinding pepper over the spaghetti.
"Er, hn hm, with respect to you two
fine kind people," he said as he
ground, "eating people is a time-
honoured custom."

Simon and Marcia quickly got to the
other side of the table. But Chair
Person only took up the fork and raked
the spaghetti into a new heap, and
ground more pepper over that. "There
were tribes in South snuffle America,"

he said, "who believed it was quite correct to – hn hm – eat their grandparents. I have a question. Is Spiggley's another word for spaghetti?"

"No," said Marcia. "It's a name."

Chair Person raked the spaghetti into a different-shaped heap and went on grinding pepper over it. "When the snuffle grandparents were dead," he said, "they cooked the grandparents and the whole tribe had a feast."

Marcia remembered seeing something like this on television. "I watched that programme too," she said.

"You – hn hm – will not know this," Chair Person said, raking the spaghetti into another new shape and grinding another cloud of pepper over it. "Only the sons and daughters of the dead men were allowed to eat the brains."

This time he spread the spaghetti flat and ground pepper very carefully over every part of it. "This was so that snuffle the wisdom of the dead man could be passed on to his family," he said.

By this time the spaghetti was grey. Simon and Marcia could not take their eyes off it. It must have been hot as fire by then. They kept expecting Chair Person to sneeze, since he seemed to have trouble breathing anyway, but he just went on grinding pepper and explaining about cannibals.

Simon wondered if Chair Person perhaps did not know how to eat. "You're supposed to put the spaghetti in your mouth," he said.

Chair Person held up the pepper mill and shook it. It was empty. So he put it down at last and picked up the

spoon. He did seem to know how to
eat, but he did it very badly, snuffling
and snorting, with ends dangling out of
his mouth. Grey juice dripped through
his smashed-hedgehog beard and ran
down his striped front. But the pepper
did not seem to worry him at all.

Simon was thinking that maybe Chair Person did not have taste buds like other people, when the back door opened and Mum and Dad came in.

"What happened to the rest of the sundial?" said Mum. "I leave you alone just for – " She saw Chair Person and stared.

"What have you kids done to those apples?" Dad began. Then he saw Chair Person and stared too.

Chapter 3

BOTH SIMON AND Marcia had had a sort of hope that Chair Person would vanish when Mum and Dad came home, or at least turn back into an armchair. But nothing of the sort happened. Chair Person stood up and bowed.

"Er, hn hm," he said. "I am Chair Person. Good snuffle evening."

Mum's eyes darted to the ink blot on Chair Person's waving sleeve, then to the coffee stain, and then on to the damp smear on his front. She turned and dashed away into the garden.

Chair Person's arms waved like someone conducting an orchestra. "I am the one causing you all this trouble with your apples," he said, in his most crawlingly humble way. "You are so kind to – hn hm – forgive me so quickly."

Dad clearly could not think what to say. After gulping a little, he said in a social sort of way, "Staying in the neighbourhood, are you?"

Here Mum came dashing back indoors. "The old chair's not in the shed any more," she said. "Do you think he *might* be – ?"

Chair Person turned to her. His arms waved as if he was a conductor expecting Mum to start singing. "Your – hn hm – husband has just made me a very kind offer," he said. "I shall be delighted to stay in this house."

"I – " Dad began.

"Er, hn hm, needless to say snuffle," said Chair Person, "I shall not cause you more trouble than I have to. Nothing more than – hn hm – a good bed and a television set in my room."

"Oh," said Mum. It was clear she could not think what to say either. "Well, er, I see you've had some supper – "

"Er, hn hm, most kind," said Chair Person. "I would love to have some supper as soon as possible. In the meantime a snuffle flask of wine would be most – hn hm – welcome. I appear to have a raging thirst."

Marcia and Simon were not surprised Chair Person was thirsty after all that pepper. They got him a carton of orange juice and a jug of water before they all hurried away to put a camp bed in Simon's room and make Marcia's bedroom ready for Chair Person. Marcia could see that Mum and Dad both had the same kind of dazed, guilty feelings about Chair Person that she had. Neither of them quite believed he was really their old armchair, but Mum put clean sheets on the bed and Dad carried the television up to Marcia's room. Chair Person seemed to get people that way.

When they came downstairs, the fridge door was open and the table was covered with empty orange juice cartons.

"I – hn hm – appear to have drunk all your orange juice," Chair Person said. "But I would be willing to drink lemon squash instead. I happen snuffle to know that it has added glucose which puts pep into the poorest parts."

He sat at the table and slurped
lemon squash while Marcia helped
Mum get supper. Simon went to look
for Dad, who was hiding behind a
newspaper in the living room. "Did
you buy a new armchair?" Simon
asked.

"Yes," said Dad. "Hush. That thing in the kitchen might get jealous."

"So you *do* believe he is the armchair!" Simon said.

"I don't *know*!" Dad groaned.

"I think he is," Simon said. "I'm quite sorry for him. It must be hard to suddenly start being a person. I expect he'll learn to speak and breathe and behave like a real person quite soon."

"I hope you're right," said Dad. "If he just learns to stop waving his arms in that spooky way I shall be quite pleased."

For supper, Chair Person ate five pizzas and six helpings of chips. In between, he waved his arms and explained, "I – hn hm – have a large appetite for my size, though I do not always need to snuffle eat. I am strange that way. Could I trouble you

41

for some Mannings' fruity brown
sauce? I appear to have eaten all your
ketchup. I think I shall enjoy my – hn
hm – life with you here. I suggest that
tomorrow we go on – hn hm – a short
tour of Wales. I think I should go to
snuffle Snowdon and then down a
coalmine."

"I'm sorry – " Dad began.

"Er, hn hm, Scotland then," said
Chair Person. "Or would you rather
charter an aeroplane and take me to
France?"

"We can't go anywhere tomorrow,"
Mum said firmly. "There's Auntie
Christa's party in the evening and the
coffee morning for Africa Aid before
that."

Chair Person did not seem at all
disappointed. He said. "I shall enjoy
that. I happen to – hn hm – know a

great deal about Africa. At the end of
the day it must be snuffle said that not
nearly enough is being done to help
Africa and the Third World. Why, in
Kenya alone . . ." And he was talking
almost word for word – apart from the
snuffles – the way last night's television
programme on Africa had talked.

Before long, Simon and Marcia had
both had enough. They tiptoed away
to Simon's room and went to bed
early.

"I suppose he's here for good,"
Simon said.

"He hasn't any other home," Marcia
said, wriggling her way into the
uncomfortable camp bed. "And he *has*
lived here for years in a sort of way. Do
you think it was the stuff that dripped
from the crystal ball that brought him
alive? Or Auntie Christa tapping him

43

with the wand? Or both?"

"Perhaps she could look after him,"
Simon said hopefully. "She does good
works. Someone's going to have to
teach him all the things that aren't on
television."

They could hear Chair Person's voice droning away downstairs. It was a loud voice, with a bleat and a bray to it, like a cow with a bad cold. After an hour or so, it was clear that Mum and Dad could not stand any more of it either. Simon and Marcia heard them coming to bed early, too. They heard Chair Person blundering upstairs after them.

"Er, hn hm – oh dear!" his voice brayed. "I appear to have broken this small table."

After that there was a lot of confused moving about and then the sound of running water. Chair Person's voice bleated out again. "Tell me – er, hn hm – is the water supposed to run all over the bathroom floor?"

They heard Mum hurry to the bathroom and turn the taps off. "There are such a lot of things he doesn't know," Marcia said sleepily.

"He'll learn. He'll be better tomorrow," Simon said.

They went to sleep, then. There was the first frost of winter that night. They woke up much earlier than they had hoped because it was so cold. Their blankets somehow seemed far too thin and there was white frost on the inside of the bedroom window. They stared at it, with their teeth chattering.

"I've never seen that before," said Simon.

"It's all feathery. It would be pretty if it wasn't so cold," said Marcia.

As she said it, they heard Dad shouting from the bathroom. "What the devil has happened to the heating boiler? It's gone *out!*"

Chair Person's feet blundered in the passage. "Er, hn hm, I appeared to get very cold in the night," his voice brayed. "But I happen to know a lot about snuffle technology. I adjusted the boiler. High speed gas for warmth and snuffle efficiency."

"It's not gas, it's *oil*!" Dad roared. "You turned the whole system off, you fool!"

"Oil?" said Chair Person, not in the least worried. "Liquid engineering. I happen to know – hn hm – that both oil and gas come from the North Sea, where giant oil rigs – "

Dad made a sort of gargling noise. His feet hammered away downstairs. There were a few clangs and a clank and the sound of Dad swearing. After a while the house started to get warm again. The frost on the window slid

48

away to the corners and turned to water.

Marcia looked at Simon. She wanted to say that Simon was the one who had said Chair Person would be better today. But she could see Simon knew he was just the same. "Do you still think he'll learn?" she said.

"I *think* so," said Simon, though he knew he was going to have to work quite hard to go on feeling sorry for Chair Person at this rate.

Chapter 4

CHAIR PERSON ATE four boiled eggs and half a packet of shredded wheat for breakfast. He drank what was left of the milk with loud slurping sounds while he told them about oil rigs and then about ship-building. "Er, hn hm," he said. "Studies at the dockyards reveal that less than ten snuffle slurp percent of ships now being built are launched by the Queen. Oh dear, I appear to have drunk all your – hn hm – milk."

50

Dad jumped up. "I'll buy more milk," he said. "Give me a list of all the other things you want for the coffee morning and I'll buy them too."

"Coward!" Mum said bitterly when Dad had gone off with orders to buy ten cake-mixes, milk and biscuits. She was in a great fuss. She told Chair Person to go upstairs and watch television. Chair Person went crawlingly humble and went away saying he knew he was – hn hm – being a lot of trouble. "And I hope he stays there!" said Mum. She made Simon help in the kitchen and told Marcia to find twenty chairs – which were all the chairs in the house – and put them in a circle in the living room. "And I suppose it's too much to hope that Auntie Christa will come in and help!" Mum added.

51

It *was* too much to hope. Auntie Christa did turn up. She put her head round the back door as Simon was fetching the sixth tray of cakes out of the oven. "I won't interrupt," she said merrily. "I have to dash down to the Community Hall. Don't forget you're all helping with the party this evening." And away she went and did not come back until Mum and Simon had heaped cakes on ten plates and Dad and Marcia were counting coffee cups. "You *have* done well!" Auntie Christa said. "We must have African Aid here every week."

Dad started to groan, and then

stopped, with a thoughtful look on his face.

The doorbell began ringing. A lot of respectable elderly ladies arrived, and one or two respectable elderly men, and then the Vicar. They each took one of the twenty seats and chatted politely while Simon and Marcia went round with cakes and biscuits and Mum handed out coffee. When everyone had a cup and a plate of something, the Vicar cleared his throat – a bit like Chair Person but nothing like so loudly.

"Er, hm," he said. "I think we should start."

The door opened just then and Dad ushered in Chair Person.

"Oh *no!*" said Mum, looking daggers at Dad.

Chair Person stood, pawing at the

air, and looked round the respectable people in a very satisfied way. He had found Dad's best shiny brown shoes to wear and Simon's football socks, which looked decidedly odd with his striped suit. The respectable people stared, at the shoes, the socks, the hairy legs above that, at the stain on his striped stomach and then at the smashed-hedgehog beard. Even Auntie Christa stopped talking and looked a little dazed.

"Er, hn hm," brayed Chair Person twice as loudly as the Vicar. "I am – hn snuffle – Chair Person. How kind of you all to come and – hn hm – meet me. These good people – " He nodded and waved arms at Dad and Mum – "have been honoured to put up with me, but they are only small stupid people who do not matter."

The slightly smug smile on Dad's face vanished at this.

"I shall – hn hm – talk to people who matter," said Chair Person. He lumbered across the room, bumping into everything he passed. Ladies hastily got coffee cups out of his way. He stopped in front of the Vicar and breathed heavily. "Could I trouble you to move?" he said.

"Eh?" said the Vicar. "Er – "

"Er, hn hm, you appear to be sitting in my seat," said Chair Person. "I am Chair Person. I am the one who shall talk to – hn hm – the Government. I shall be running this meeting."

The Vicar got out of the chair as if it had scalded him and backed away. Chair Person sat himself down and looked solemnly round.

"Coffee," he said. "Er, hn hm, cakes.

While the rest of the world starves."

Everyone shifted and looked uncomfortably at their cups.

In the silence, Chair Person looked at Mum. "Hn hm," he said. "Maybe you have not noticed that you've not given me – hn hm – coffee or cakes."

"Is *that* what you meant?" said Mum. "I thought after all the breakfast you ate – "

"I meant – hn hm – that we are here to feast and prove that we at least have enough to eat," said Chair Person. While Mum was angrily pouring coffee into the cracked cup that was the last one in the cupboard, he turned to the nearest lady. "I decided to grow a beard," he said, "to show I am – hn hm – important to the ecology. It makes my face look snuffle grand."

The lady stared at him. Auntie

56

Christa said loudly, "We are here to
talk about Africa, Mr Chair Person."

"Er, hn hm," said Chair Person. "I
happen to know a lot about Africa.
The Government should act to make

sure that the African – hn hm –
elephant does not die out."

"We were not going to talk about
elephants," the Vicar said faintly.

"The snuffle gorilla is an endangered
animal too," said Chair Person. "And
the herds of – hn hm – wildebeeste are
not what they were in the days of Dr
Livingstone, I presume. Drought
afflicts many animals – I appear to
have drunk all my coffee – and famine
is poised to strike." And he went on
talking, mixing up about six different
television programmes as he talked.
The Vicar soon gave up trying to
interrupt, but Auntie Christa kept
trying to talk too. Every time she
began, Chair Person went "ER,
HNHM!" so loudly that he drowned
her out, and took no notice of anything
she said. Marcia could not help

thinking that Chair Person must have stood in the living room picking up hints from Auntie Christa for years. Now he was better at not letting other people talk than Auntie Christa was.

In the meantime, Chair Person kept eating cakes and asking for more coffee. The respectable people, in a dazed sort of way, tried to keep up with Chair Person, which meant that Simon and Marcia were kept very busy carrying cups and plates. In the kitchen Mum was baking and boiling the kettle non-stop, while Dad grimly undid packets and mixed cake-mix after cake-mix.

By this time Simon was finding it hard to be sorry for Chair Person at all. "I didn't know you thought you were so important," he said as he brought Chair Person another plate of steaming buns.

"This must be – hn hm – reported to Downing Street," Chair Person told the meeting, and he interrupted himself to say to Simon, "That is because I – er, hn hm – always take care to be polite to people like you who don't snuffle count . . . I shall make you feel good by praising these cakes. They are snuffle country soft and almost as mother used to make." And turning back to the dazed meeting, he said, "Ever since the days of the Pharoahs – hn hm – Egypt has been a place of snuffle mystery and romance."

There seemed nothing that would ever stop him. Then the doorbell rang. Unfortunately, Dad, Mum, Marcia and Simon were all in the kitchen when it rang, pouring the last of the cake-mix into paper cases. By the time

Marcia and Dad got to the front door, Chair Person had got there first and opened it.

Two men were standing outside holding a new armchair. It was a nice armchair, a nice plain blue, with a pleasant look on the cushion at the back where Chair Person's face had come from. Marcia thought Mum and Dad had chosen well.

"I – er, hn hm – I said take that thing away," Chair Person told the men. "This house is not big enough for snuffle both of us. The post is – hn hm – filled. There has been a mistake."

"Are you sure? This is the right address," one of the men said.

Dad pushed Chair Person angrily aside. "Mind your own business!" he said. "No, there's no mistake. Bring that chair inside."

Chair Person folded his waving arms. "Er, hn hm. My rival enters this house over my dead body," he said. "This thing is bigger than snuffle both of us."

While they argued, Auntie Christa was leading the coffee morning people in a rush to escape through the kitchen and out of the back door. "I do think," the Vicar said kindly to Mum as he scampered past, "that your eccentric uncle would be far happier in a Home, you know."

Mum waited until the last person had hurried through the back door. Then she burst into tears. Simon did not know what to do. He stood staring at her. "A Home!" Mum wept. "I'm the one who'll be in a Home if someone doesn't *do* something!"

Chapter 5

CHAIR PERSON got his way over the
new chair, more or less. The men
carried it to the garden shed and
shoved it inside. Then they left,
looking almost as bewildered and
angry as Dad.

Marcia, watching and listening, was
quite sure now that Chair Person had
been learning from Auntie Christa all
these years. He knew just how to make
people do what he wanted. But Auntie
Christa did not live in the house. You
could escape from her sometimes.
Chair Person seemed to be here to
stay.

"We'll have to get him turned back into a chair somehow," she said to Simon. "He's not getting better. He's getting worse and worse."

Simon found he agreed. He was not sorry for Chair Person at all now. "Yes, but *how* do we turn him back?" he said.

"We could ask old Mr Pennyfeather," Marcia suggested. "The conjuring set came from his shop."

So that afternoon they left Mum lying on her bed upstairs and Dad moodily picking up frost-bitten apples from the grass. Chair Person was still eating lunch in the kitchen.

"Where does he put it all?" Marcia wondered as they hurried down the road.

"He's a chair. He's got lots of room

for stuffing," Simon pointed out.

Then they both said. "Oh *no!*" Chair Person was blundering up the road after them, panting and snuffling and waving his arms. "Er, hn hm, wait for me!" he called out. "You appear to have snuffle left me behind."

He tramped beside them, looking pleased with himself. When they got to the shops where all the people were, shoppers turned to stare as Chair Person clumped past in Dad's shoes. Their eyes went from the shoes, to the football socks, and then to the short, striped suit, and then on up to stare wonderingly at the smashed-hedgehog beard. More heads turned every time Chair Person's voice brayed out, and of course he talked a lot. There was something in every shop to set him going.

At the bread shop, he said, "Er, hn hm, those are Sam Browne's lusty loaves. I happen to know snuffle they are nutrition for the nation."

Outside the supermarket, he said, "Cheese to please, you can snuffle freeze it squeeze it and – er, hn hm – there is Tackley's Tea which I happen to know has over a thousand holes to every bag. Flavour to snuffle savour."

Outside the wine shop his voice went up to a high roar. "I – hn hm – see Sampa's Superb sherry here which

is for ladies who like everything silken snuffle smooth. And I happen to know that in the black bottle there is – hn hm – a taste of Olde England. There is a stagecoach on the – hn hm – label to prove it. And look, there is Bogans – hn hm – Beer which is of course for Men Only."

By now it seemed to Simon and Marcia that everyone in the street was staring. "You don't want to believe everything the ads say," Simon said uncomfortably.

"Er, hn hm, I appear to be making you feel embarrassed," Chair Person brayed, louder than ever. "Just tell me snuffle if I am in your way and I will snuffle go home."

"Yes, do," they both said.

"I – er, hn hm – wouldn't dream of pushing in where I am snuffle not wanted," Chair Person said. "I would – hn hm – count it a favour if you tell me snuffle truthfully every time you've had enough of me. I – er, hn hm – know I must bore you quite often."

By the time he had finished saying this they had arrived at old Mr Pennyfeather's junk shop. Chair Person stared at it.

"We – er, hn hm – don't need to go in there," he said. "Everything in it is old."

"You can stay outside then," said
Marcia.

But Chair Person went into another
long speech about not wanting to be –
hn hm – a trouble to them and
followed them into the shop. "I – er,
hn hm – might get lost," he said, "and
then what would you do?"

He bumped into a cupboard.

Its doors opened with a *clap* and a
stream of horse brasses poured out:
clatter, *clatter*, CLATTER!

Chair Person lurched sideways from
the horse brasses and walked into an
umbrella stand made out of an
elephant's foot,

which fell over – *crash* CLATTER –

against a coffee table with a big jug
on it,

which tipped and slid the jug off –

69

CRASH, splinter, splinter –

and then fell against a ricketty
bookcase,

which collapsed sideways, spilling
books – thump, thump, thump-thump-
thump –

and hit another table loaded with
old magazines and music,

which all poured down around
Chair Person.

It was like dominoes going down.

The bell at the shop door had not
stopped ringing before Chair Person
was surrounded in knocked-over
furniture and knee-deep in old papers.
He stood in the midst of them, waving
his arms and looking injured.

By then, Mr Pennyfeather was on
his way from the back of the shop,
shouting, "Steady, steady, steady!"

"Er, hn hm – er, hn hm," said Chair

Person, "I appear to have knocked one or two things over."

Mr Pennyfeather stopped and looked at him, in a knowing, measuring kind of way. Then he looked at Simon and Marcia. "He yours?" he said. They nodded. Mr. Pennyfeather nodded too. "Don't move," he said to Chair Person. "Stay just where you are."

Chair Person's arms waved as if he was conducting a very large orchestra, several massed choirs and probably a brass band or so as well. "I – er, hn hm, er, hn hm – I – er, hn hm – " he began.

Mr Pennyfeather shouted at him. "*Stand still! Don't move, or I'll have the springs out of you and straighten them for toasting forks*! It's the only language they understand," he said to Simon

and Marcia. "STAND STILL! YOU
HEARD ME!" he shouted at Chair
Person.

Chair Person stopped waving his arms and stood like a statue, looking quite frightened.

"You two come this way with me," said Mr Pennyfeather, and he took Simon and Marcia down to the far end of his shop, between an old ship's wheel and a carved maypole, where there was an old radio balanced on a tea chest. He turned the radio up loud so that Chair Person could not hear them. "Now," he said, "I see you two got problems to do with that old conjuring set. What happened?"

"It was Auntie Christa's fault," said Marcia.

"She let the crystal ball drip on the chair," said Simon.

"*And* tapped it with the magic wand," said Marcia.

Mr Pennyfeather scratched his

withered old cheek. "My fault, really," he said. "I should never have let her have those conjuring things, only I'd got sick of the way the stuff in my shop would keep getting lively. Tables dancing and such. Mind you, most of my furniture only got a drip or so. They used to calm down after a couple of hours. That one of yours looks as though he got a right dousing – or maybe the wand helped. What was he to begin with, if you don't mind my asking?"

"Our old armchair," said Simon.

"Really?" said Mr Pennyfeather. "I'd have said he was a sofa, from the looks of him. Maybe what you had was an armchair with a sofa opinion of itself. That happens."

"Yes, but how can we turn him *back*?" said Marcia.

Mr Pennyfeather scratched his withered cheek again. "This is *it*," he said. "Quite a problem. The answer must be in that conjuring set. It wouldn't make no sense to have that crystal ball full of stuff to make things lively without having the antidote close by. That top hat never got lively. You could try tapping him with the wand again. But you'd do well to sort through the box and see if you couldn't come up with whatever was put on the top hat to stop it getting lively at all."

"But we haven't got the box," said Simon. "Auntie Christa's got it."

"Then you'd better borrow it back off her quick," Mr Pennyfeather said, peering along his shop to where Chair Person was still standing like a statue. "Armchairs with big opinions of theirselves aren't no good. That one could turn out a real menace."

"He already *is*," said Simon.

Marcia took a deep grateful breath and said, "Thanks awfully, Mr Pennyfeather. Do you want us to help tidy up your shop?"

"No, you run along," said Mr Pennyfeather. "I want him out of here before he does any worse." And he shouted down the shop at Chair Person, "Right, you can move now! Out of my shop *at* the double and wait in the street!"

Chair Person nodded and bowed in his most crawlingly humble way and waded through the papers and out of the shop. Simon and Marcia followed, wishing they could manage to shout at Chair Person the way Mr Pennyfeather had. But maybe they had been brought up to be too polite. Or maybe it was

Chair Person's sofa opinion of himself.
Or maybe it was just that Chair
Person was bigger than they were and
had offered to eat them when he first
came out of the shed. Whatever it was,
all they seemed to be able to do was to
let Chair Person clump along beside
them, talking and talking, and try to
think how to turn him into a chair
again.

They were so busy thinking that
they had turned into their own road
before they heard one thing that Chair
Person said. And that was only
because he said something new.

"*What* did you say?" said Marcia.

"I said," said Chair Person, "I
appear – er, hn hm, snuffle – to have
set fire to your house."

Both their heads went up with a
jerk. Sure enough, there was a fire

engine standing in the road by their gate. Firemen were dashing about unrolling hoses. Thick black smoke was rolling up from behind the house, darkening the sunlight and turning their roof black.

Simon and Marcia forgot Chair Person and ran.

Mum and Dad, to their great relief, were standing in the road beside the fire engine, along with most of the neighbours. Mum saw them. She let go of Dad's arm and rushed up to Chair Person.

"All right. Let's have it," she said. "What did you do *this* time?"

Chair Person made bowing and hand-waving movements, but he did not seem sorry or worried. In fact, he was looking up at the surging clouds of black smoke rather smugly. "I – er, hn

hm – was thirsty," he said. "I appear
to have drunk all your orange juice
and lemon squash and the stuff snuffle

from the wine and whisky bottles, so I
– hn hm – put the kettle on the gas for
a cup of tea. I appear to have forgotten
it when I went out."

"You fool!" Mum screamed at him.
"It was an electric kettle, anyway!"
She was angry enough to behave just
like Mr Pennyfeather. She pointed a
finger at Chair Person's striped
stomach. "I've had enough of you!"
she shouted. "You stand there and
don't *dare* move! Don't *stir*, or I'll – I'll
– I don't know what I'll do but you
won't like it!"

And it worked, just like it did when
Mr Pennyfeather shouted. Chair
Person stood still as an overstuffed
statue. "I – hn hm – appear to have
annoyed you," he said in his most
crawlingly humble way.

He stood stock still in the road all

the time the firemen were putting out
the fire. Luckily only the kitchen was
burning. Dad had seen the smoke
while he was picking up apples in the
garden. He had been in time to phone
the Fire Brigade and get Mum from
upstairs before the rest of the house
caught fire. The firemen hosed the
blaze out quite quickly. Half an hour
later, Chair Person was still standing
in the road and the rest of them were
looking round the ruined kitchen.

Mum gazed at the melted cooker,
the crumpled fridge and the charred
stump of the kitchen table. Everything
was black and wet. The vinyl floor had
bubbled. "Someone get rid of Chair
Person," Mum said, "before I murder
him."

"Don't worry. We're going to,"
Simon said soothingly.

"But we have to go and help at Auntie Christa's Children's party in order to do it," Marcia explained.

"I'm not going," Mum said. "There's enough to do here – and I'm not doing another thing for Auntie Christa – not after this morning!"

"Even Auntie Christa can't expect us to help at her party after our house has been on fire," Dad said.

"Simon and I will go," Marcia said. "And we'll take Chair Person and get him off your hands."

Chapter 6

THE SMOKE HAD made everything in the
house black and gritty. Simon and
Marcia could not find any clean
clothes, but the next door neighbours
let them use their bathroom and kindly
shut up their dog so that Marcia would
not feel nervous. The neighbours the
other side invited them to supper when
they came back. Everyone was very
kind. More kind neighbours were
standing anxiously round Chair Person
when Simon and Marcia came to fetch
him. Chair Person was still standing
like a statue in the road.

"Is he ill?" the lady from Number 27 asked.

"No, he's not," Marcia said. "He's just eccentric. The Vicar says so."

Simon did his best to imitate Mr Pennyfeather. "Right," he barked at Chair Person. "You can move now. We're going to a party."

Though Simon sounded to himself just like a nervous person talking loudly, Chair Person at once started snuffling and waving his arms about. "Oh – hn hm – good," he said. "I believe I shall like a party. What snuffle party is it? Conservative, Labour or that party whose name keeps changing? Should I be – hn him – sick of the moon or over the parrot?"

At this, all the neighbours nodded to one another. "*Very* eccentric," the lady from Number 27 said as they all went away.

Simon and Marcia led Chair Person towards the Community Hall trying to explain that it was a party for Caring Society Children. "And we're supposed to be helping," Marcia said. "So do you think you could try to behave like a proper person for once?"

"You – hn hm – didn't have to say *that*!" Chair Person said. His feelings were hurt. He followed them into the hall in silence.

The hall was quite nicely decorated with bunches of balloons and full of children. Simon and Marcia knew most of the children from school. They were surprised they needed caring for – most of them seemed just ordinary children. But the thing they looked at mostly was the long table at the other end of the room. It had a white cloth on it. Much of it was covered with food: jellies, cakes, crisps and big bottles of coke. But at one end was the pile of prizes, with the green teddy on top. The conjuring set, being quite big, was at the bottom of the pile. Simon and Marcia were glad, because that would mean it would be the last prize anybody won. They would have time to look through the box.

Auntie Christa was in the midst of the children, trying to pin someone's torn dress. "There you are at last!" she called to Simon and Marcia. "Where are your mother and father?"

"They couldn't come – we're awfully sorry!" Marcia called back.

Auntie Christa rushed out from among the children. "Couldn't come? Why *not*?" she said.

"Our house has been on fire – "

Simon began to explain.

But Auntie Christa, as usual, did not listen. "I think that's extremely thoughtless of them!" she said. "I was counting on them to run the games. Now I shall have to run them myself."

While they were talking, Chair Person lumbered into the crowd of children, waving his arms importantly.

"Er, hn hm, welcome to the party," he brayed. "You are all honoured to have me here because I am – snuffle – Chair Person and you are only children who need caring for."

The children stared at him resentfully. None of them thought of themselves as needing care. "Why is he wearing football socks?" someone asked.

Auntie Christa whirled round and stared at Chair Person. Her face went quite pale. "Why did you bring *him*?" she said.

"He – er – he needs looking after," Marcia said, rather guiltily.

"He just nearly burnt our house down," Simon tried to explain again.

But Auntie Christa did not listen. "I shall speak to your mother very crossly indeed!" she said and ran back among

the children, clapping her hands.
"Now listen, children. We are going to
play a lovely game. Stand quiet while I
explain the rules."

"Er, hn hm," said Chair Person.
"There appears to be a feast laid out
over there. Would it snuffle trouble
you if I started eating it?"

At this, quite a number of the
children called out, "Yes! Can we eat
the food now?"

Auntie Christa stamped her foot.
"No you may *not*! Games come first.
All of you stand in a line and Marcia
bring those bean bags from over
there."

Once Auntie Christa started giving
orders, Chair Person became quite
obedient. He did his best to join in the
games. He was hopeless. If someone
threw him a bean bag, he dropped it.

If he threw a bean bag at someone else, it hit the wall or threatened to land in a jelly. The team he was in lost every time.

So Auntie Christa tried team Follow My Leader and that was even worse. Chair Person lost the team he was with and galumphed round in small circles on his own. Then he noticed that everyone was running in zig-zags and ran in zig-zags too. He zagged when everyone else zigged, bumping into people and treading on toes.

"Can't you stop him? He's spoiling the *game!*" children kept complaining.

Luckily, Chair Person kept drifting off to the table to steal buns or help himself to a pint or so of coke. After a while, Auntie Christa stopped rounding him up back into the games. It was easier without him.

But Simon and Marcia were getting worried. They were being kept so busy helping with teams and fetching things and watching in case people cheated that they had no time at all to get near the conjuring set. They watched the other prizes go. The green teddy went first, then the broken train, and then other things, until half the pile was gone.

Then at last Auntie Christa said the next game was Musical Chairs. "Simon and Marcia will work the record player and I'll be the judge," she said. "All of you bring one chair each into the middle. *And* you!" she said, grabbing Chair Person away from where he was trying to eat a jelly. "This is a game even you can play."

"Good," Simon whispered as he and Marcia went over to the old, old record player. "We can look in the box while the music's going."

Marcia picked up an old scratched record and set it on the turntable. "I thought we were never going to get a chance!" she said. "We can give them a good long go with the music first time." She carefully lowered the lopsided stylus. The record began:

Here we go gathering click *in May,*
Click *in May, nuts in* click . . .

and all the children danced cautiously round the chairs, with Chair Person prancing in their midst, waving his arms like a lobster.

Simon and Marcia ran to the table and pulled the conjuring box out from under the other prizes. The crystal ball was still leaking. There was quite a damp patch on the tablecloth. But the wand was lying on top, when they opened the box, still wrapped in flags. Simon snatched it up. Marcia ran back and lifted the stylus off the record. There was a stampede for chairs.

Chair Person of course was the one without a chair. Simon had expected that. He followed Chair Person and gave him a smart tap with the wand as Chair Person blundered up the line of sitting children. But the wand did not seem to work. Chair Person pushed the smallest girl off the end chair and sat in it himself.

"I saw that! You were out!" Auntie Christa shouted, pointing at him.

Chair Person sat where he was. "I – er, hn hm – appear to be sitting in a chair," he said. "That was the snuffle rule as I understand it."

Auntie Christa glared. "Start the game again," she said.

Simon tapped Chair Person on the
head with the wand before everyone
got up, but that did not seem to work
either. "What shall we *do*?" he
whispered to Marcia, as they hurried
back to the record player.

"Try it without the flags," Marcia
whispered back. She lowered the stylus
again.

Here we go gathering click *in May*, the

record began as Simon dashed over to the table, unwrapping the string of flags from the wand as he went. He was just putting the flags back in the box, when the table gave a sort of wriggle and stamped one of its legs.

Simon beckoned Marcia madly. The box must have been standing on the table for quite a long time. The stuff from the crystal ball had leaked down into the table and spread along the tablecloth to the food. The tablecloth was rippling itself, in a sly, lazy way. As Marcia arrived, one of the jellies spilt its way up to the edge of its cardboard bowl and peeped timidly out.

"It's *all* getting lively," Simon said.

"We'd better take the crystal ball to the toilet and drain it away," Marcia said.

"No!" said Simon. "Think what might happen if the toilet gets lively! Think of something else."

"Why should *I* always have to be the one to think?" Marcia snapped. "Get an idea for yourself for once!" She knew this was unfair, but by this time she was in as bad a fuss as Mum.

Here the record got as far as *Who shall we* click *to* click *him away?* and stuck. *Who shall we* click, *who shall we* click . . .

Marcia raced for the record and took it off. Simon raced among the stampede towards Chair Person and hit him with the unwrapped wand. Again nothing happened. Chair Person pushed a boy with a leg-brace off the end chair and sat down. Auntie Christa said angrily, "This is *too* bad! Start the game again."

Marcia put the stylus down on the
beginning of the record a third time.
"I'd better stay and do this," she said.
"You go and search the box – quickly,
before we get landed with Table
Person and Jelly Person as well!"

Simon sped to the table and started
taking things out of the conjuring box
– first the flags, then the dripping hat
with the crystal ball in it. After that
came a toy rabbit, which was perhaps
meant to be lively when it was fetched
out of the hat. Yet, for some reason, it
was just a toy. None of the things in
the box was more than just wet. Simon
took out a sopping leather wallet, three
soaking packs of cards, and a dripping
bundle of coloured handkerchiefs.
They were all just ordinary. That
meant that there *had* to be a way of
stopping things getting lively, but

search as he would, Simon could not find it.

As he searched, the cracked music stopped and started and the table stamped one leg after another in time to it. Simon glanced at the game. Chair Person had found another way to cheat. He simply sat in his chair the whole time.

"I'm counting you out," Auntie Christa kept saying. And Chair Person went on sitting there with his smashed-hedgehog chin pointing obstinately to the ceiling.

Next time Simon looked, there were only two chairs left beside Chair Person's and three children. "We'll have tea after this game," Auntie Christa called as Marcia started the music again.

Help! thought Simon. The wobbling,

climbing jelly was half out of its bowl,
waving little feelers. Simon turned the
whole box out on to the jigging table.
All sorts of things fell out. But there
was nothing he could see that looked
useful – except perhaps a small wet
pillbox. There was a typed label on its
lid that said DISAPPEARING BOX.

Simon hurriedly opened it.

It was empty inside, so very empty that he could not see the bottom. Simon put it down on the table and stared into it, puzzled.

Just then, the table got livelier than ever from all the liquid Simon had emptied out of the conjuring box. It started to dance properly. The tablecloth got quite lively too and stretched itself in a long, lazy ripple. The two things together rolled the hat with the crystal in it across the tiny, empty pillbox.

There was a soft WHOP. The hat and the crystal were sucked into the box. And they were gone. Just like that. Simon stared.

The table was still dancing and the tablecloth was still rippling. One by one, and very quickly, the other things from the conjuring box were rolled and jigged across the tiny pillbox. WHOP went the rabbit, WHOP the wand, WHOP-WHOP the string of flags, and then all the other things WHOP WHOP WHOP, and they were all gone too. The big box that had held the things tipped over and made a bigger *WHOP*. And that was gone as well, before Simon could move. After that the other prizes started to vanish WHOP WHOP WHOP. This seemed to interest the tablecloth. It put out a long, exploring corner towards the pillbox.

At that, Simon came to his senses. He pushed the corner aside and rammed the lid on the pillbox before the tablecloth had a chance to vanish too.

As soon as the lid was on, the

pillbox was not there any more. There was not even a whisper of a WHOP as it went. It was just gone. And the tablecloth was just a tablecloth, lying half wrapped across the few prizes left. And the table stood still and was just a table. The jelly slid back into its bowl. Its feelers were gone and it was just a jelly.

The music stopped too. Auntie Christa called out, "Well done, Philippa! You've won again! Come and choose a prize, dear."

"It's not fair!" somebody complained. "Philippa's won *everything*!"

Marcia came racing over to Simon as he tried to straighten the tablecloth. "Look, look! You *did* it! Look!"

Simon turned round in a dazed way. There were still two chairs standing in

the middle of the hall after the game.
One of them was an old shabby striped
armchair. Simon was sure that was not
right. "Who put – ?" he began. Then
he noticed that the chair was striped in
sky-blue, orange and purple. Its
stuffing was leaking in a sort of fuzz
from its sideways top cushion. It had
stains on both arms and on the seat.

Chair Person was a chair again. The only odd thing out was that the chair was wearing football socks and shiny shoes on its two front legs.

"I'm not sure if it was the wand or the pillbox," Simon said.

They pushed the armchair over against the wall while everyone was crowding round the food.

"I don't think I could bear to have it on our bonfire after this," Marcia said. "It wouldn't seem quite kind."

"If we take its shoes and socks off," Simon said, "we could leave it here. People will probably think it belongs to the Hall."

"Yes, it would be quite useful here," Marcia agreed.

Later on, after the children had gone and Auntie Christa had locked up the hall, saying over her shoulder, "Tell your mother and father that I'm not on speaking terms with either of them!" Simon and Marcia walked slowly home.

Simon asked, "Do you think he knew we were going to put him on our bonfire? Was he having his revenge on us?"

"He may have been," said Marcia. "He never talked about the bonfire, did he? But what was to stop him just *asking* us not to when he was a person?"

"No," said Simon. "He didn't have to set the house on fire. I suppose that shows the kind of Person he was."

Some other Young Puffins

RADIO RESCUE
John Escott

Mia is enjoying her holiday with her father by the seaside, away from her mother who is always criticizing her for not reading and writing well. But Mia's reading difficulties lead her into all sorts of trouble when she ignores the Danger sign.

MICHAEL AND THE JUMBLE-SALE CAT
Marjorie Newman

Michael lives in the children's home with his best friend Lee and his precious jumble-sale cat. One day Jenny, his social worker, asks if he'd like to live with a new family and Michael is thrown into confusion, but when the day arrives for him to leave the children's home he is both sad and glad. His new family turn out to be very special indeed!

ANOTHER BIG STORY BOOK
Richard Bamberger

One of the foremost experts of literature for children has collected here some of the world's most enchanting and magical fairy tales. From the English tale 'Jack and the Beanstalk' to the Indian 'Wali Dad the Simple', these are stories parents will enjoy telling and children will remember with pleasure for the rest of their lives.

DUSTBIN CHARLIE

Ann Pilling

Charlie had always liked seeing what people threw out in their dustbins. So he's thrilled to find the toy of his dreams among the rubbish in the skip. But during the night, someone else takes it. The culprit in this highly enjoyable story turns out to be the most surprising person.

CLASS THREE AND THE BEANSTALK

Martin Waddell

Two unusual stories which will amaze you. Class Three's project on growing things gets out of hand after they plant a packet of Jackson's Giant Bean seeds. And when Wilbur Small is coming home, the whole street is buzzing – except for Tom Grice and his family, who are new in the street so don't know what the fuss is about, or why people are so nervous!

THE TWIG THING

Jan Mark

As soon as Rosie and Ella saw the house they knew that something was missing. It had lots of windows and stairs, but where was the garden? When they move in, they find a twig thing which they put in water on the window-sill, and gradually things begin to change.

HELP!

Margaret Gordon

Fred and Flo are very helpful little pigs. The problem is, the more helpful they try to be, the more trouble they cause. Whether they are washing Grandad's car, looking after Baby or doing the decorating, disaster is never far away! Four hilarious stories featuring two very charming – and helpful – piglets.

DUMBELLINA

Brough Girling

What could be worse than the thought of moving house, changing school and leaving all your friends behind? When her Mum announces they are moving, Rebecca feels totally miserable – until she meets Dumbellina, the iron fairy.

ENOUGH IS ENOUGH

Margaret Nash

Usually when Miss Boswell uses her magic phrase, it works: Class 1 know that she means enough is *enough*, and get back to work, for a while at least. But when Miss Boswell's special plant begins to grow and grow until it has wiped the sums off the board, curled right out of the classroom and is heading for the kitchen, not even shouting 'Enough is enough!' will stop it!